FLOWER·FAIRIES
OF·THE·AUTUMN

FLOWER·FAIRIES
OF·THE·AUTUMN

With the nuts and berries they bring

Poems and pictures by
CICELY MARY BARKER

◆

FREDERICK WARNE

The reproductions in this book have been made using the most modern electronic scanning methods from entirely new transparencies of Cicely Mary Barker's original watercolours. They enable Cicely Mary Barker's skill as an artist to be appreciated as never before.

FREDERICK WARNE
Published by the Penguin Group
27 Wrights Lane, London W8 5TZ, England
Penguin Books USA Inc., 375 Hudson Street, New York, N.Y. 10014, USA
Penguin Books Australia Ltd, Ringwood, Victoria, Australia
Penguin Books Canada Ltd, 10 Alcorn Avenue, Toronto, Ontario, Canada M4V 3B2
Penguin Books (NZ) Ltd, 182-190 Wairau Road, Auckland 10, New Zealand

Penguin Books Ltd, Registered Offices: Harmondsworth, Middlesex, England

First published 1926
This edition with new reproductions first published 1990

ISBN 0 7232 3755 7

Colour reproduction by
Anglia Graphics Limited, Bedford
Printed and bound in Great Britain by
William Clowes Limited, Beccles and London

0496

•CONTENTS•

SEE ABOVE THE FAIRY'S
HEAD, GUELDER-ROSE'S
BERRIES RED.

◆ THE BERRY-QUEEN ◆

An elfin rout,
　　With berries laden,
Throngs round about
　　A merry maiden.

Red-gold her gown;
　　Sun-tanned is she;
She wears a crown
　　Of bryony.

The sweet Spring came,
　　And lovely Summer:
Guess, then, her name—
　　This latest-comer!

The Mountain Ash Fairy

◆ THE SONG OF ◆
THE MOUNTAIN ASH FAIRY

They thought me, once, a magic tree
   Of wondrous lucky charm,
And at the door they planted me
   To keep the house from harm.

They have no fear of witchcraft now,
   Yet here am I today;
I've hung my berries from the bough,
   And merrily I say:

"Come, all you blackbirds, bring your wives,
   Your sons and daughters too;
The finest banquet of your lives
   Is here prepared for you."

(The Mountain Ash's other name is Rowan; and it used to
be called Witchentree and Witch-wood too.)

◆ THE SONG OF ◆
THE MICHAELMAS DAISY FAIRY

"Red Admiral, Red Admiral,
   I'm glad to see you here,
      Alighting on my daisies one by one!
I hope you like their flavour
   and although the Autumn's near,
      Are happy as you sit there in the sun?"

"I thank you very kindly, sir!
   Your daisies *are* so nice,
      So pretty and so plentiful are they;
The flavour of their honey, sir,
   it really does entice;
      I'd like to bring my brothers, if I may!"

"Friend butterfly, friend butterfly,
   go fetch them one and all!
      I'm waiting here to welcome every guest;
And tell them it is Michaelmas,
   and soon the leaves will fall,
      But *I* think Autumn sunshine is the best!"

The Michaelmas Daisy Fairy

The Wayfaring Tree Fairy

◆ THE SONG OF ◆
THE WAYFARING TREE FAIRY

My shoots are tipped with buds as dusty-grey
As ancient pilgrims toiling on their way.

Like Thursday's child with far to go, I stand,
All ready for the road to Fairyland;

With hood, and bag, and shoes, my name to suit,
And in my hand my gorgeous-tinted fruit.

◆ THE SONG OF ◆
THE ROBIN'S PINCUSHION FAIRY

People come and look at me,
Asking who this rogue may be?
—Up to mischief, they suppose,
Perched upon the briar-rose.

I am nothing else at all
But a fuzzy-wuzzy ball,
Like a little bunch of flame;
I will tell you how I came:

First there came a naughty fly,
Pricked the rose, and made her cry;
Out I popped to see about it;
This is true, so do not doubt it!

The Robin's Pincushion Fairy

The Elderberry Fairy

◆ THE SONG OF ◆
THE ELDERBERRY FAIRY

Tread quietly:
O people, hush!
—For don't you see
A spotted thrush,
One thrush or two,
Or even three,
In every laden elder-tree?

They pull and lug,
They flap and push,
They peck and tug
To strip the bush;
They have forsaken
Snail and slug;
Unseen I watch them, safe and snug!

(These berries do us no harm, though they don't taste very nice. Country people make wine from them; and boys make whistles from elder stems.)

◆ THE SONG OF ◆
THE ACORN FAIRY

To English folk the mighty oak
   Is England's noblest tree;
Its hard-grained wood is strong and good
   As English hearts can be.
And would you know how oak-trees grow,
   The secret may be told:
You do but need to plant for seed
   One acorn in the mould;
For even so, long years ago,
   Were born the oaks of old.

The Acorn Fairy

The Dogwood Fairy

◆ THE SONG OF ◆
THE DOGWOOD FAIRY

I was a warrior,
   When, long ago,
Arrows of Dogwood
   Flew from the bow.
Passers-by, nowadays,
   Go up and down,
Not one remembering
   My old renown.

Yet when the Autumn sun
   Colours the trees,
Should you come seeking me,
   Know me by these:
Bronze leaves and crimson leaves,
   Soon to be shed;
Dark little berries,
   On stalks turning red.

(Cornel is another name for Dogwood; and Dogwood has
nothing to do with dogs. It used to be Dag-wood, or Dagger-
wood, which, with another name, Prickwood, show that it was
used to make sharp-pointed things.)

◆ THE SONG OF ◆
THE BLACK BRYONY FAIRY

Bright and wild and beautiful
For the Autumn festival,
I will hang from tree to tree
Wreaths and ropes of Bryony,
To the glory and the praise
Of the sweet September days.

(There is nothing black to be seen about this Bryony, but
people do say it has a black root; and this may be true, but you
would need to dig it up to find out. It used to be thought a cure
for freckles.)

The Black Bryony Fairy

The Horse Chestnut Fairy

◆ THE SONG OF ◆
THE HORSE CHESTNUT FAIRY

My conkers, they are shiny things,
    And things of mighty joy,
And they are like the wealth of kings
    To every little boy;
I see the upturned face of each
    Who stands around the tree:
He sees his treasure out of reach,
    But does not notice *me*.

For love of conkers bright and brown,
    He pelts the tree all day;
With stones and sticks he knocks them down,
    And thinks it jolly play.
But sometimes I, the elf, am hit
    Until I'm black and blue;
O laddies, only wait a bit,
    I'll shake them down to you!

◆ THE SONG OF ◆
THE BLACKBERRY FAIRY

My berries cluster black and thick
For rich and poor alike to pick.

I'll tear your dress, and cling, and tease,
And scratch your hands and arms and knees.

I'll stain your fingers and your face,
And then I'll laugh at your disgrace.

But when the bramble-jelly's made,
You'll find your trouble well repaid.

The Blackberry Fairy

The Nightshade Berry Fairy

◆ THE SONG OF ◆
THE NIGHTSHADE BERRY FAIRY

"You see my berries, how they gleam and
     glow,
Clear ruby-red, and green, and orange-
     yellow;
Do they not tempt you, fairies, dangling so?"
    The fairies shake their heads and answer "No!
      You are a crafty fellow!"

"What, won't you try them? There is
     naught to pay!
Why should you think my berries poisoned
     things?
You fairies may look scared and fly away—
The children will believe me when I say
     My fruit is fruit for kings!"
    But all good fairies cry in anxious haste,
  "O children, do not taste!"

(You must believe the good fairies, though the berries look
nice. This is the Woody Nightshade, which has purple and
yellow flowers in the summer.)

◆ THE SONG OF ◆
THE ROSE HIP FAIRY

Cool dewy morning,
  Blue sky at noon,
White mist at evening,
  And large yellow moon;

Blackberries juicy
  For staining of lips;
And scarlet, O scarlet
  The Wild Rose Hips!

Gay as a gipsy
  All Autumn long,
Here on the hedge-top
  This is my song.

The Rose Hip Fairy

The Crab-Apple Fairy

◆ THE SONG OF ◆
THE CRAB-APPLE FAIRY

Crab-apples, Crab-apples, out in the wood,
Little and bitter, yet little and good!
The apples in orchards, so rosy and fine,
Are children of wild little apples like mine.

The branches are laden, and droop to the
    ground;
The fairy-fruit falls in a circle around;
Now all you good children, come gather
    them up:
They'll make you sweet jelly to spread
    when you sup.

One little apple I'll catch for myself;
I'll stew it, and strain it, to store on a shelf
In four or five acorn-cups, locked with a key
In a cupboard of mine at the root of the tree.

◆ THE SONG OF ◆
THE HAZEL-NUT FAIRY

Slowly, slowly, growing
    While I watched them well,
See, my nuts have ripened;
    Now I've news to tell.
I will tell the Squirrel,
    "Here's a store for you;
But, kind Sir, remember
    The Nuthatch likes them too."

I will tell the Nuthatch,
    "Now, Sir, you may come;
Choose your nuts and crack them,
    But leave the children some."
I will tell the children,
    "You may take your share;
Come and fill your pockets,
    But leave a few to spare."

The Hazel-Nut Fairy

The White Bryony Fairy

◆ THE SONG OF ◆
THE WHITE BRYONY FAIRY

Have you seen at Autumn-time
　Fairy-folk adorning
All the hedge with necklaces,
　Early in the morning?
Green beads and red beads
　Threaded on a vine:
Is there any handiwork
　Prettier than mine?

(This Bryony has other names—White Vine, Wild Vine, and
Red-berried Bryony. It has tendrils to climb with, which Black
Bryony has not, and its leaves and berries are quite different.
They say its root is white, as the other's is black.)

♦ THE SONG OF ♦
THE BEECHNUT FAIRY

O the great and happy Beech,
 Glorious and tall!
Changing with the changing months,
 Lovely in them all:

Lovely in the leafless time,
 Lovelier in green;
Loveliest with golden leaves
 And the sky between,

When the nuts are falling fast,
 Thrown by little me—
Tiny things to patter down
 From a forest tree!

(You may eat these.)

The Beechnut Fairy

The Hawthorn Fairy

◆ THE SONG OF ◆
THE HAWTHORN FAIRY

These thorny branches bore the May
　　So many months ago,
That when the scattered petals lay
　　Like drifts of fallen snow,
　　"This is the story's end," you said;
　　But O, not half was told!
For see, my haws are here instead,
And hungry birdies shall be fed
　　On these when days are cold.

◆ THE SONG OF ◆
THE PRIVET FAIRY

Here in the wayside hedge I stand,
And look across the open land;
Rejoicing thus, unclipped and free,
I think how you must envy me,
O garden Privet, prim and neat,
With tidy gravel at your feet!

(In early summer the Privet has spikes of very strongly-scented white flowers.)

The Privet Fairy

The Sloe Fairy

◆ THE SONG OF ◆
THE SLOE FAIRY

When Blackthorn blossoms leap to sight,
They deck the hedge with starry light,
    In early Spring
    When rough winds blow,
    Each promising
    A purple sloe.

And now is Autumn here, and lo,
The Blackthorn bears the purple sloe!
    But ah, how much
    Too sharp these plums,
    Until the touch
    Of Winter comes!

(The sloe is a wild plum. One bite will set your teeth on
edge until it has been mellowed by frost; but it is not poisonous.)

Also by Cicely Mary Barker
The Lord of the Rushie River
Simon the Swan